W9-BLG-414

CAN YOU PROTECT THE CORAL REEFS?

AN INTERACTIVE ECO ADVENTURE

BY MICHAEL BURGAN

CAPSTONE PRESS
a capstone imprint

You Choose Books are published by Capstone Press, an imprint of Capstone.
1710 Roe Crest Drive
North Mankato, Minnesota 56003
www.capstonepub.com

**Library of Congress Cataloging-in-Publication data is available on the Library
of Congress website.**
ISBN 978-1-4966-9597-0 (library binding)
ISBN 978-1-4966-9705-9 (paperback)
ISBN 978-1-9771-5393-7 (eBook PDF)

Summary: Pollution, climate change, and overfishing are killing the world's coral
reefs. But you can help! Navigate through three different stories in this ecological
rescue mission.

Photo Credits
Dreamstime/Colin Moore, 59; Getty Images: GIANRIGO MARLETTA,
79, Miami Herald, 50; Newscom: Howard Lipin, 42, Yang Guanyu Xinhua
News Agency, 90; Science Source: David Vaughan, 26, Jessica Wilson, 106-107;
Shutterstock: Afanasiev Andrii, 54, Andrey Armyagov, cover, (top), 1 (t), aquapix,
29, Dan Logan, 46, Ethan Daniels, 12, 100-101, 104-105, Ian Scott, 93, Karel
Bartik, 96, Keat Eung, 63, Kristina Vackova, 34, Lewis Burnett, 70, muratart,
20, Ocean Image Photography, 74, rangizzz, cover (b), backcover (t), 1 (b), 4,
S.Bachstroem, 67, SARAWUT KUNDEJ, 17, Simon Dannhauer, 6, superjoseph,
98, UnderTheSea, 39, Vlad61, 83, Vorayooth Panakul, 87

Artistic elements: Shutterstock: Natali Snailcat

Editorial Credits
Editor: Michelle Parkin; Designer: Bobbie Nuytten; Media Researcher:
Kelly Garvin; Production Specialist: Katy LaVigne

TABLE OF CONTENTS

ABOUT YOUR ADVENTURE

YOU are a researcher trying to save the tropical coral reefs from extinction. You and a team of scientists are racing to save them. Can you help make a difference before it's too late?

Chapter One sets the scene. Then you choose which path to read. Follow the directions at the bottom of the page as you read the stories. The decisions you make will change your outcome. After you finish one path, go back and read the others for new perspectives and more adventures.

Turn the page to begin your adventure.

CHAPTER 1

TRAVELING TO CARRIE BOW

After a long day's travel from the United States, you sit in a small motorboat plowing through crystal-clear water. Ahead, you see a small area of sand. Several buildings sit on this tiny island, and palm trees sway in the warm breeze. It looks like paradise. But you're not here for a vacation.

A few minutes later, you reach Carrie Bow Cay. The island is off the mainland of Belize. At Carrie Bow, scientists and other researchers are trying to save natural wonders that many people never see—coral reefs.

Turn the page.

You're a researcher who specializes in marine biology. You've spent years in your lab, studying coral reefs. And now, you can't believe your luck. You have the chance to study these reefs up close, in their natural habitat. You hope that with your knowledge and skills, you'll be able to help save the reefs that surround Carrie Bow and other islands around the world.

You know how important coral reefs are. They cover less than two percent of the ocean bottoms, yet they provide food and shelter to about 25 percent of the world's marine species. Fishers catch and sell the fish living in the reefs. Coral reefs also protect coastal lands from the devastating impact of huge storms, like hurricanes.

And tourists pay to visit the colorful reefs. This provides jobs for people who live near the reefs.

But the world's coral reefs are facing extinction. Rising ocean temperatures caused by climate change are killing them.

"It's not just ocean temperatures that we worry about," Dr. Samantha Johnson tells you. She is one of the scientists who spends several months each year at Carrie Bow Cay. "People dump pollution into the waters. Or they want to build on islands near the reefs, or they damage them while they fish. All of those things threaten the reefs."

"What can I do to help?" you ask Dr. Johnson.

Turn the page.

She explains that she has three different scientific projects for you to choose from. You will be going with several other researchers. The first is on an island in the middle of the Pacific Ocean.

The second is aboard a research ship called the *Seahorse*. It will be studying reefs in the Atlantic Ocean, off the coast of the United States.

The last option isn't research. A team of biologists are going to Hawaii to head up a cleanup effort. Pollution there has damaged the coral reefs. The research team is hoping that cleaning up the reef will allow it to begin to heal and repair itself.

"None of them are easy," she explains.

"But all of them are important. Your work can help us better understand life in the reefs—and how we can save them."

To see coral reefs up close in the Pacific Ocean, turn to page 13.

To explore deep-water reefs on the *Seahorse*, a research ship at sea, turn to page 47.

To clean up coastal reefs, turn to page 71.

CHAPTER 2

REEFS AT DIFFERENT DEPTHS

Dr. Johnson tells you that the work in the Pacific Ocean will take place in the waters around Palau. Palau is a small island nation about 550 miles east of the Philippines. It's made up of more than 300 small islands.

Only one other researcher has chosen to go to Palau. His name is Sandeep. On the flight to Palau, Sandeep talks about the coral reefs there.

"I was in Palau before, studying coral bleaching," he tells you. "There are about 700 kinds of corals there. They're amazing."

Bleaching is a huge problem for coral reefs. Rising water temperatures or other conditions destroy the colorful algae living inside the reef.

Turn the page.

Rising temperatures force the reef to push out the algae. The reef turns white, like a skeleton, and slowly starves. Some reefs can survive the bleaching. But most don't. You know that more than half of the Great Barrier Reef in Australia has died because of massive coral bleaching.

After several flights and many hours in the air, you and Sandeep finally reach Palau. At the airport, a woman standing by a small van waves to you. She walks over.

"Welcome to Palau," the woman says. "My name is Carol. I help run the Coral Reef Research Center here."

Carol takes you and Sandeep to a small building along the shore. Inside, you meet several scientists who are doing research in Palau. Two of them are eager to tell you about their projects.

One of them is Dr. Stanley Katz, a professor of marine sciences.

"My team wants to learn why some coral reefs survive better in warm water than others," Dr. Katz tells you. "These reefs live in shallow water, so we don't need scuba gear to explore them. We just use snorkels."

The other scientist is Dr. Sheila Armstrong. She tells you, "My work focuses on reefs that are up to 500 feet deep. This is the ocean's mesophotic layer. Only limited sunlight can reach that far down into the ocean."

"Both Dr. Armstrong and Dr. Katz could use your help," Carol tells you. "Which kind of reef would you like to explore?"

To join Dr. Katz's team and snorkel in the shallow reefs, turn to page 16.

To be on Dr. Armstrong's team and explore the mesophotic reefs, turn to page 28.

Dr. Katz tells you to put away your suitcase and get down to the dock.

"You're just in time for our first dive of the day," he says.

You get onto the small boat that will take you out to the reef. Then you put on your snorkeling gear. Dr. Katz explains that you'll help collect samples of corals of different species from different areas of the reef.

"Then we'll study them in the lab," he says. "Some species of coral reefs are dying because of the heat. If we can learn which coral species survive increased water temperatures, we can focus our rescue efforts on them. We could transport some of those to start new colonies."

The boat stops, and you dive into the water. You've never seen water so clear. It's easy to spot the reef below. Tiny fish are all around it.

You carefully remove small pieces of different kinds of coral. You take your samples back to the boat, then jump back in the water to find more.

Turn the page.

Thriving coral reefs support countless types of marine life.

Soon Dr. Katz signals that it's time to go back to the research center. When you arrive, Carol is waiting for you.

"How was it?" she asks.

"It was incredible!" you say.

"Good," Carol says. "Now I have another project for you, if you're up for it. Follow me."

Carol leads you down to the dock. You see a man standing next to what looks like a small torpedo. "This is Dr. Sidney Kulis," Carol says. "He's working with one of our AUVs."

AUV stands for autonomous underwater vehicle. Unlike a remotely operated vehicle (ROV), an AUV is not connected to a ship. It follows a path that scientists program into it. AUVs are useful for studying coral reefs and other parts of the ocean.

"This is the Remus 100," Dr. Kulis explains. "It collects data, such as the water temperature or how much oxygen is in the water. It can find objects underwater using sonar. And we can put cameras on it to see what it encounters."

Dr. Kulis goes on. "With Remus, we've discovered new coral reefs here in Palau. I'm going to look for more reefs today."

You and Dr. Kulis lower the AUV into the water. He sets some controls, and then the AUV begins to slowly cruise away. As it gets farther from shore, you watch it go under the surface.

In the van, Carol sets up the video screen that will let you see what Remus finds. The farther down Remus goes, the darker the screen gets. But there is still enough light to see fish swimming by. You see coral reefs too.

Turn the page.

"Anything new yet?" you ask Dr. Kulis.

He shakes his head no. "But pretty soon."

Carol has been outside the van on the phone. She pokes her head inside.

"I have some bad news," Carol says. "It looks like there's a thunderstorm coming. And it could be a big one."

Lighting strikes are rare on the ocean, but when they happen, they can kill fish and damage boats.

"Hmm, that is bad news," Dr. Kulis says. "We'll need to cut the mission short."

"I don't know if Remus will make it back before the storm hits," Carol says. "Could we leave it underwater until the storm is over?"

"Maybe we should go out in a boat to get it back," Dr. Kulis says. He turns to you. "Would you go out with me to get Remus? Or do you think it's too dangerous?"

To go retrieve the AUV with Dr. Kulis, turn to page 22.
To suggest letting it ride out the storm, turn to page 25.

You follow Dr. Kulis to a small motorboat. As you both climb in, you can see dark storm clouds getting nearer. The wind begins to whip harder. On the water, bigger and bigger waves begin to rock the boat.

"I've already sent a signal to Remus," Dr. Kulis says. "It's beginning to come back toward the surface. We should be able to get to it in a few minutes."

You notice that the seas are getting rougher. All you can think about is getting back to shore. Soon, you see the thin, yellow body of the AUV.

"There it is!" you shout.

Dr. Kulis turns the boat toward it. Rain pelts your face, and you hear a rumble of thunder.

"Do you think we'll make it back before the storm gets worse?" you ask.

"I'm sure we can get Remus in time," Dr. Kulis says. "But it could be a rough ride back to shore."

He pulls the boat closer to the AUV. You each grab a handle on top of the machine and haul it up onto the boat.

"Safe and sound," he says with a smile. "Now, let's get out of here."

Dr. Kulis turns the boat around and heads for the island. You see lightning not far away, and the thunder is getting louder. The rain and the spray of the waves soaks you to the bone. Another flash of lightning makes you jump. It does not feel safe being on the water during this storm.

Finally, as the rain pours down even harder, you see the shore just ahead.

Turn the page.

"We made it," Dr. Kulis says. "Were you getting worried?"

You smile a bit. "Just a little."

Back on land, you help Dr. Kulis get the AUV into the van. You hope the storm ends soon so you can get back to work looking for coral reefs.

THE END

To read another adventure, turn to page 11.
To learn more about Coral Reefs, turn to page 99.

"Maybe we should stay in the van," you say.

Dr. Kulis nods in agreement. "We can see if Remus keeps sending a video signal," he says. "And as soon as the storm is over, we'll go get it."

Carol joins you and Dr. Kulis in the van. Through the windshield, you see the skies darken. Then the rain comes pouring down. Bolts of lightning fill the sky. On the video screen, you see Remus is bouncing around from the powerful waves. Then the screen goes dark.

"That can't be good," you say.

Dr. Kulis frowns. "I don't know. It could just be a problem with the video. We'll see."

The storm gets stronger. You feel the wind begin to rock the van. Carol keeps adjusting the controls to see if she can get the video back.

Turn the page.

Finally, the wind starts to fade a bit. The rain gets lighter. Almost as quickly as the storm blew in, it's passed by.

"Carol, try to bring Remus up the surface," Dr. Kulis says. Then he says to you, "Let's go to where it should be."

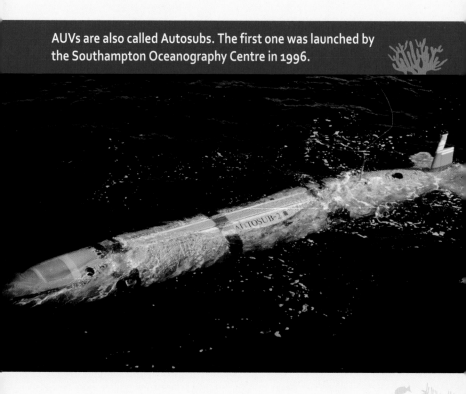

AUVs are also called Autosubs. The first one was launched by the Southampton Oceanography Centre in 1996.

You and Dr. Kulis climb into a small motorboat. The sea is still choppy, but not as rough as it was just minutes before. After a while, Carol comes out of the van and waves for you to come back in.

"I think we lost it," Carol says. "There isn't any signal at all from Remus."

It will take months to get another AUV out into the water. You know how disappointed Dr. Kulis must be knowing that his important research will be delayed. Maybe you should have gotten the AUV out of the water before the storm hit, but would it have been worth the risk?

THE END

To read another adventure, turn to page 11.
To learn more about Coral Reefs, turn to page 99.

"Have you ever gone scuba diving before?" Dr. Armstrong asks you.

"Yes, many times," you say.

Scuba diving is one way to explore the mesophotic corals. They're very different from the ones close to the water's surface. Mesophotic corals are usually soft, and they don't form big colonies like the corals in shallow waters.

"We've been exploring the mesophotic reefs for more than 20 years," Dr. Armstrong says. "We want to save all reefs. And these might be especially useful. We think the chemicals in some of them could be used to make medicine."

Dr. Armstrong leads you to a spot on the dock where other researchers are putting on scuba gear.

Turn the page.

"We use special equipment to dive down," she explains. "Divers have much larger air tanks than usual. And they use the rebreather method."

The rebreather method allows the diver to breathe the same air twice, after the carbon dioxide is removed from the exhale. You've made dives using that system for years.

"We also have a small submersible," Dr. Armstrong says.

She waves for you to follow her. She stops by a small vehicle a little more than 8 feet long. On top is a plastic dome, and in front are two mechanical arms.

"It's called the Deepworker 2000," she says. "A single person can use it to go down almost 2,000 feet and collect samples. With the sub, we can stay underwater for up to 80 hours."

"Wow, that's incredible!" you say.

"Would you like to scuba dive or use the submersible?" Dr. Armstrong asks.

To explore a reef with the Deepworker, turn to page 32.

To scuba dive down to a reef, turn to page 36

Over the next several days, Dr. Armstrong teaches you how to pilot the Deepworker. You control the tiny sub's movements with foot pedals. That leaves your hands free to operate the video camera and the mechanical arms.

"With the arm, you'll cut off tiny samples of the coral," Dr. Armstrong says. "Then we'll study them here at the research center."

After a lot of training, you're ready to pilot the Deepworker. Dr. Armstrong tells you to explore one of the mesophotic reefs and bring back samples. You open the plastic hatch and climb into the submersible. Your heart is racing. Once you go down, you'll be alone. You'll be in radio contact with the research center. But it won't be like your training dives, when people were always close by.

A crane lowers the Deepworker into the water. Then you begin to go down. As the sea darkens, you turn on the sub's outside light. You can see that the corals here are different from the ones near the surface. They look more like plants. You grab the control of one of the arms to pick up a rock with some corals on it. You turn the camera toward a rock. Now Dr. Armstrong can see what you've found too.

"That's a beauty," she says over the radio.

You spend several hours exploring and getting coral samples. As you begin to head up, you see several creatures swimming toward you. You realize they're squids.

"Don't worry about them," Dr. Armstrong says. "They're more afraid of you than you are of them."

Turn the page.

You're not sure what you think. But you don't want the scientists to think that you're afraid.

Suddenly, the water is filled with a green cloudy ink.

The common reef squid is often found near coral reefs.

"One of the squids is shooting its ink at me!" you tell Dr. Armstrong.

"They're just trying to scare you away," she says. "Swing around them and keep coming up."

Soon, the squids are out of sight. You make it back to the surface and open the hatch. Dr. Armstrong is waiting for you.

"Excellent job," she says.

You're proud of your work in the Deepworker. And you know the samples you collected will help the team better understand mesophotic coral reefs and find ways to save them. You can't wait to get into the water again.

THE END

To read another adventure, turn to page 11.
To learn more about Coral Reefs, turn to page 99.

Dr. Armstrong leads you over to the researchers getting ready to dive. You see Sandeep, the researcher you met on the trip to Palau.

"You're going down too?" he asks.

You nod. "I just have to get my suit and gear."

"I'll wait for you," Sandeep says.

You go into the research center and get your equipment. Back on the dock, you join Sandeep. The two of you dive into the water. As you dive, you see the different reefs. You also see some that are bleached. It's heart-wrenching. You will do all you can to save the corals here.

You continue to explore. The deeper you go, the darker it gets. Lights that you've brought along help you see.

For this dive, your assignment is to collect some of the fish that live in the mesophotic reefs. Some of these fish have just been recently discovered. Scientists want to know more about them. They also hope that by finding the new species, people around the world will be more interested in protecting mesophotic reefs.

It takes just a few minutes for you and Sandeep to reach the bottom of the dive. You both go to explore a nearby reef.

"Let's collect some fish on this side," Sandeep says, pointing to the left side of the reef.

You notice that Sandeep's voice sounds funny—it's much higher than usual. He sounds like a little kid.

"Ok," you say. "But why do you sound like that?"

Turn the page.

"One of the gases we're breathing in is helium. It's also used to blow up party balloons," he says. "It's safe but can change our voices."

Sandeep catches a fish swimming through the reef. He puts it in a special container you're holding. It'll take time for the fish to adjust to living on the surface after being so deep underwater. The container will make sure the fish stays alive.

Sandeep looks at his watch and points up to the surface. You can only stay this deep underwater for about 10 minutes. Now, it's time to go back up. The trip back will take hours. You have to go up slowly. The gases you breathe are now in your blood. If you go up too quickly, some of the gases could turn to bubbles. This is very dangerous. It can shut off the flow of blood.

Turn the page.

Two scuba divers swim near a coral reef teeming with fish and sea anemones (bottom right).

If that happens, your brain or other organs could be damaged. You could even die. On your way up to the surface, you rest several times.

About 100 feet from the surface, Sandeep says, "Something's wrong. My head hurts, and I feel dizzy."

These are signs that his rebreather is not working correctly. Sandeep could be in real trouble. He needs help. You could continue going toward the surface for help. But should you leave him alone in the water?

To go to the surface alone, go to page 41.
To stay with Sandeep, turn to page 44.

You don't want to leave Sandeep alone when he's in trouble. But you have to get help. If his rebreather isn't working, he could die.

You take off for the surface of the water. But you're going a little too fast. You worry about how your body will react. You start to feel some pain in your joints. Divers call it the bends. You try not to think about that. The most important thing is helping Sandeep.

Finally, you reach the surface. Dr. Armstrong is surprised to see you. She knows it should have taken longer for you to come up safely.

"Sandeep needs help," you say. "I think his rebreather is malfunctioning."

Dr. Armstrong and Carol pull you out of the water.

Turn the page.

Researchers release a robotic submarine into the ocean.

"We have the Deepworker sub ready to go out," Dr. Armstrong says. "I'll have the pilot bring down another unit and find Sandeep. The sub can stay with him until he makes it back."

"And you should go to the hospital," Carol says. "The doctors there can check you out. You may need oxygen."

You nod as she helps you take off your scuba gear. Then she takes you over to the van. As you drive away, you hope you'll be able to dive again on this trip. But more importantly, you hope Sandeep is ok. You can only imagine how much pain he is in right now.

THE END

To read another adventure, turn to page 11.
To learn more about Coral Reefs, turn to page 99.

It's a risk not to go for help. But you don't want to leave Sandeep alone in the water.

"Are all your gas levels set right?" you ask him.

"I'm not sure," Sandeep says.

You go over and look at the small computer on Sandeep's wrist. It controls the amount of oxygen he gets. The levels are too high.

"I'm going to reset your gas levels," you tell him.

Sandeep is alert, but you can see that he's getting weak. You need to move quickly to save him.

"I'm going to help you go up to the surface," you tell Sandeep. You put your arm around his waist and slowly begin to rise. You know you can't go too fast, or you both could be in danger. Finally, you see the surface above you.

"You're doing ok?" you ask Sandeep.

He nods. "But I should probably go to the hospital just in case."

You help Sandeep over to Dr. Armstrong. She calls for the van to bring Sandeep to the hospital. You realize now that diving so deep can be dangerous. But all the scientists are willing to take that risk to try to save the reefs.

THE END

To read another adventure, turn to page 11.
To learn more about Coral Reefs, turn to page 99.

CHAPTER 3

DIVING DEEP

You've always wanted to go out on a research ship. Another researcher named Amy joins you on this mission. Dr. Johnson explains to both of you that a research team is about to explore part of the coast of the Eastern United States.

"There's an area from the tip of Florida to southern Virginia that is filled with deep-sea corals," Johnson tells you. "But in large parts of that region, we don't know exactly what kind of corals live where. You two will join our team to look for and explore new reefs."

The next day, you leave Carrie Bow Cay and head for Massachusetts. That's the home of the *Seahorse*, a 275-foot long research ship.

Turn the page.

The *Seahorse* will take you out to sea. On board, you spot a white vessel with an orange top.

"I wonder what that is," you say, pointing to the vessel.

"You don't know?" Amy says. "That's Fred!"

"That's right," a man behind you says. You turn and see him approaching. He introduces himself as Dr. Steve Cook. He's one of the scientists on the *Seahorse*. "Fred is a submersible," Dr. Cook says.

You learn that the sub can travel more than 3 miles underwater and stay there for up to 10 hours. Inside, scientists use its robotic arms to pick up pieces of coral.

"That's incredible," Amy says.

"Just wait until you see Nemo," Dr. Cook says with a smile. "That's our remotely operated vehicle, or ROV. It's like a small, underwater robot that we can control here on the ship."

As you walk, you can't help but be amazed at all the technology the scientists have on board. You can't wait to use it. You follow Dr. Cook into the lab.

"I'd like to introduce you to the scientists in the lab," he says. "You'll be working with them to preserve the samples of coral reef and other sea life we collect."

You see rows of bottles labeled with the names of different kinds of coral. You've never seen so many coral species.

Turn the page.

Scientists in Florida are collecting coral samples to try to save the reefs from being killed off.

"Collecting coral samples is just one of the jobs we do," says Dr. Sarah Strauss, another scientist on board. "From the deck, we drop instruments into the water to measure the salt content and temperature. We also collect water samples to study the tiny sea creatures that are food for fish around the reefs.

Dr. Cook turns to you. "Would you like to collect water samples or get a closer look at Nemo?"

To work on deck, turn to page 52.
To see Nemo, turn to page 56.

"I'd like to work with you on the deck, Dr. Strauss," you say.

The next day, Dr. Strauss leads you to a device a few feet taller than you.

"This is called a CTD," she explains. It has a round metal frame. All around the frame are plastic bottles. "These will collect the water samples," she goes on, pointing to the bottles. "And at the bottom of the CTD is the electrical equipment that takes measurements."

Dr. Strauss introduces you to the crew that will put the CTD in the ocean. The skies are gray. While the sea is not as rough as it was overnight, you still see large swells of water.

You turn to the crew leader, "Is it safe to launch this in such rough seas?"

"We have to be careful," he says. "The cables can get twisted. And if the CTD breaks loose, we'll lose some pretty expensive equipment."

The CTD is attached to a winch that lowers it into the water. But before the winch can lower the CTD down, a huge wave hits the *Seahorse*. You see the CTD swing wildly to the right, and then to the left—directly at one of the scientists.

"Look out!" you cry.

Without thinking, you dive and push him down. You both tumble to the deck, the CTD swinging just above you. A sudden wave sends the ship rolling. You watch with horror as the scientist slides overboard. You see a life preserver nearby and toss it into the water.

Turn the page.

"Grab it!" you yell.

The scientist swims for the preserver. Then, you and the crew members begin to pull him in.

"We've almost got you!" you say.

You reach to pull the man onto the ship. Dripping with water, the scientist lies on the deck. He looks up at you. "Thank you."

Life preservers and flotation devices can help keep people afloat in the water while they're being rescued.

"That was quick thinking," Dr. Strauss says. "That's a good skill to have when we're out at sea."

Dr. Strauss tells the CTD crew to stop for today. "We'll try again tomorrow," she says.

You haven't done any research yet, but you feel you've already done something important on this voyage.

THE END

To read another adventure, turn to page 11.
To learn more about Coral Reefs, turn to page 99.

"I'd love to get a closer look at Nemo," you say to Dr. Cook.

Amy decides to collect water samples with Dr. Strauss. Dr. Cook takes you out on deck and introduces you to Roger, the engineer in charge of keeping both Fred and Nemo running smoothly. Then you get your first look at Nemo. It's about 3 feet long, with two metal arms in front that are attached to a cylinder.

"We're testing out Nemo on this trip," Roger explains. "We want to shrink the lionfish population."

"Why?" you ask.

"Certain fish protect the reefs by controlling the amount of seaweed and algae around. But lionfish eat these helpful fish. No other fish eat the lionfish, so their population keeps growing."

"How will Nemo help?" you ask.

"We can guide Nemo to the areas where the lionfish live," Roger says. "Our goal is to catch some of the lionfish and sell them to fish markets. ROVs like Nemo are cheap. In the future, fishers could buy their own ROVs and then sell what they catch. They'll help reduce the lionfish population, and the coral reefs will be protected."

Dr. Cook brings you over to the team preparing to launch Fred. Leading them is Dr. Aleisha Davis.

"We're hoping to find some species of coral polyps that we've never seen before," Dr. Davis explains. "It promises to be an exciting trip."

Turn the page.

Dr. Cook says, "So, which would you like to do—work with Nemo or go down into the ocean in Fred?"

You like the idea of stopping lionfish from damaging reefs. But finding new polyps could lead to new ways to save these and other reefs.

To work with Nemo, go to page 59.
To go in Fred, turn to page 66.

"Let's go catch some lionfish and try to save a reef," you say excitedly.

Dr. Cook takes you back to Roger, who explains a little more about how Nemo works.

"We control Nemo from the ship using a joystick, similar to what you would use to play a video game," Roger explains. "We receive video images from Nemo's onboard camera."

Turn the page.

An ROV is launched from a ship.

"How do you collect the lionfish?" you ask.

Dr. Cook points to small panels at the end of each metal arm at the front of the ROV.

"Those panels send out a small electrical jolt," he says. "It just stuns the fish. Then Nemo collects them. On a good trip, we can catch about 10 fish."

Roger leads you into a small room on the *Seahorse* with the controls for Nemo. Some crew members have already put the ROV into the water. On a video screen, you see what Nemo sees with its camera. It dives down at about 100 feet per minute.

After a few minutes, you begin to see some lionfish in the water. Roger guides the ROV toward one. He presses a button to send the electrical current into the panels.

Soon, the fish has been collected by the ROV.

Roger points at the joystick and asks, "Would you like to give it a try?"

You'd love to try working the ROV, but you've never controlled one before. You'd hate to damage such important equipment.

To control Nemo, turn to page 62.
To just watch, turn to page 64.

"I'm pretty good with video games," you say with a smile. "So, I should do all right with this."

You move Nemo around with the joystick and soon spot a lionfish. You carefully move Nemo toward the fish. Then, you push the button that sends the electrical current into the panels. With the push of another button, Nemo sucks the fish inside.

You and Roger take turns catching lionfish until Nemo is filled with all it can hold.

"Ok, let's bring Nemo back up," he says.

Roger lets you guide the ROV back to the surface. In a few minutes you're out on deck, watching the crew haul Nemo out of the water. Through its clear plastic body, you see the stunned fish are moving again.

Lionfish have fins that fan out like the mane of a male lion.

You know that with fewer lionfish in the water, you're helping to protect the coral reefs. You're glad to have even a small part in this important work.

THE END

To read another adventure, turn to page 11.
To learn more about Coral Reefs, turn to page 99.

You decide to observe as Roger searches for another lionfish. Nemo is now near some underwater cliffs. Roger carefully steers the ROV alongside them.

"There's one," you say, pointing to a corner of the video screen.

You watch as Nemo moves toward the fish. It darts inside a crack in the cliff. Nemo moves closer. You see the fish inside.

"Let's see if I can get it out of there," Roger says.

He swings the front of Nemo toward the cliff. One of its arms knocks against the rock. The fish doesn't move. Roger swings the ROV again. This time, you see an arm break off one of the panels.

"That's not good," Roger says under his breath. He moves Nemo away from the cliff.

"Can it be fixed?" you ask.

"Hopefully," Roger says as he begins to bring Nemo toward the surface. "We'll know once we see the damage up close."

But one thing is for sure. Today's fishing expedition is over. You're just grateful you weren't the one to break such an expensive machine. You hope Nemo is repaired before your time at sea comes to an end.

THE END

To read another adventure, turn to page 11.
To learn more about Coral Reefs, turn to page 99.

You and Dr. Davis climb into Fred. The pilot is already inside. She shakes your hand, then shows you to your seat. The three of you share a cockpit that is barely 7 feet wide.

"We collect most of our samples on the left side," Dr. Davis says, "so the lead scientist always sits there. You'll sit on the other side and take notes on what depth we're at and what you see."

In less than 20 minutes, Fred is about 1,500 feet underwater. Sunlight doesn't reach that deep, so the submersible has its own lights. You can't believe you're seeing this amazing undersea world up close.

Finally, Fred reaches the bottom of the ocean. Then, it begins to slowly go back up near a rocky wall 200 feet high. You see coral growing over the edges of the rocks.

Turn the page.

An ROV inspects coral growing out of a shipwreck.

"Most of these coral are short because of the strong ocean currents down here," Dr. Davis says. "We're the first people to see these corals."

The pilot brings Fred up the left side of the rocky wall. Dr. Davis directs it toward a coral to take a sample.

As the submersible inches closer, you hear Dr. Cook's voice over the radio.

"Fred, come in," he says. "How is it going down there?"

"Everything's fine," the pilot says. "We're making our way up the left side of the wall."

"Fred, come in. Do you hear me?" Dr. Cook says again.

"Dr. Cook, come in. Do you copy?" the pilot replies.

You wait to hear a response, but the radio is silent.

"Is something wrong with the radio?" you ask.

"It appears to be," the pilot says. "I'm sorry, Dr. Davis. We have to follow protocol. If the ship can't contact us, we have to end the mission."

"I'm sorry," Dr. Davis says to you. "It looks like this sample will be the only one we'll get this time."

Your first dive is over before it really began. You just hope you'll be able to go down again before the *Seahorse* heads home.

THE END

To read another adventure, turn to page 11.
To learn more about Coral Reefs, turn to page 99.

CHAPTER 4

OCEAN CLEANUP

"I'm glad you're interested in the cleanup work," Dr. Johnson says. "Pollution in the water is a major threat to coral reefs."

She tells you she is planning to leave for Hawaii the next day.

"The state is doing cleanup work in Kaneohe Bay. And some scientists are doing work there with super corals."

"I'd like you to come along with me," Dr. Johnson says. "But there's also an opening on another scientist's team. They're leaving for a cleanup mission in Singapore."

"Fascinating!" you exclaim. "I've never seen coral reefs so close to a huge city."

Turn the page.

"It is huge," Dr. Johnson says. "But it's on an island and has many smaller islands around it. There are certainly plenty of coral reefs there."

You're curious to learn about super corals. But Singapore also sounds exciting. And it would be good to try to protect reefs in such a highly populated area.

To go to Hawaii with Dr. Johnson's team, go to page 73.

To go to Singapore with the other scientist's team, turn to page 86.

After spending the night in Carrie Bow Cay, you and Dr. Johnson make the long trip to Hawaii. As you travel, Dr. Johnson tells you more about the corals there.

"About 5,000 different kinds of plants and sea creatures live in Hawaii's reefs," she says. "Some of them aren't found anywhere else in the world. That's one of the reasons why it's so important to protect the reefs here."

You finally reach the Hawaiian island of Oahu. Kaneohe Bay is on the eastern side of the island. You head to Coconut Island, which is in the bay. It's home to a marine research center.

At the center, Dr. Johnson introduces you to several other scientists.

"This is Sam Tanaka," Dr. Johnson says. "He's working on super coral reefs."

Turn the page.

"And this is Linda Cousins," Dr. Johnson says. "She's trying to repair reefs that have already been damaged. Both Linda and Sam could use another researcher with your talents on their team. Where would you like to work?"

To work on damaged reefs, go to page 75.
To work on super coral reefs, turn to page 78.

Fish swim along coral reefs near Hawaii.

"I'm happy to have you aboard," Linda says. "Let's get right to work,"

She takes you outside and gives you some snorkeling equipment. In the bay, she points to a barge.

"That's where we keep the vacuum," she says. "Come on, I'll show you how it works."

Linda puts on a dive suit and scuba gear, and you put on yours. Just a few feet down, you see a reef. Linda dives in and picks up a large hose in the water. She signals to the barge, and you hear a whooshing sound. You watch as the hose begins to suck up seaweed in the water. After about 30 seconds, the hose goes off. You and Linda come up to the surface again.

"All that seaweed hurts the reefs," Linda says. "It blocks the sunlight the corals need to live."

Turn the page.

"But don't all reefs have some seaweed around them?" you ask.

"This seaweed is different," Linda explains. "It's not native to our waters. It was brought here to harvest a chemical inside it. But the seaweed grew too fast, and the local fish can't eat enough of it to protect the reefs."

"So, you use the vacuum to help clean up the reefs?" you ask.

"Yes, but that's just the first step," Linda says.

She leads you into a small building near the shore. Inside are tanks filled with sea creatures.

"Sea urchins?" you ask, puzzled.

"That's right," Linda says. "We raise them in a lab on another part of the island, then release them around the reefs. They eat the seaweed, so it doesn't grow back."

You head back out to the water. Linda carries a whole tray of the urchins. You swim out to the reef and watch her put some of the urchins on the coral. She motions for you to do the same thing. Soon, the two of you are spreading out the urchins. When you're done, you head back to shore.

Linda tells you the marine research center has plenty more urchins to place at sea. You'll be able to keep protecting Hawaii's reefs for at least another week.

THE END

To read another adventure, turn to page 11.
To learn more about Coral Reefs, turn to page 99.

"I'll take you to see the super coral now," Sam tells you.

You follow Sam to a small boat. Inside, you see scuba gear. Sam tells you to put on a diving suit. Then, he heads the boat out into the bay.

"Decades ago, people here put their waste into the bay," Sam explains. "They stopped about 40 years ago. But by then, almost all of the coral reefs were destroyed by the pollution."

"That's terrible," you say.

"But there is some good news," Sam continues. "Over time, some of the reefs came back to life. And what's amazing is the water here is warmer and more acidic than in other spots. Scientists didn't think the corals could live in these conditions. That's why they're called super corals."

Turn the page.

Scientists in Florida have grown pillar coral in tanks. Many of them have died of disease in the wild.

Your mission here is to learn how super corals can survive in the harsh conditions. One day, these corals could be moved and used to build new reefs in other warm or acidic waters.

After going about 500 yards, Sam stops the boat.

"We're close to the patch reefs. There are two in this area. We can head left or right. What do you think?"

To tell Sam to go left, go to page 81.
To tell him to go right, turn to page 83.

The boat quickly reaches the patch reef. You strap on your oxygen tank and fins and put on your mask. You follow Sam into the water.

The reef is not too deep. Soon you see the colorful corals. But there are some white spots too. Even super coral can experience bleaching and die. You watch Sam cut off samples from both the healthy and dying coral to study them back at the marine center.

It's exciting to see so many kinds of coral up close. As you swim, you notice all the fish that live in there. But after a few minutes, you begin to feel dizzy. Sam sees you stop swimming and comes over to you. He pulls out a dive slate to write a message to you.

"Are you ok?" it says.

You shake your head no.

Turn the page.

Sam hands you the slate and you write, "Dizzy."

Sam points to the surface. You know he wants you go back up right away. With Sam right beside you, you return to the surface. You take off your mask and suck in big gulps of air.

"I bet the mask wasn't on properly," Sam said. "You're lucky we hadn't gone too deep."

"I know," you say, still gasping for fresh air.

You're already starting to feel better. You can't wait for another chance to explore the super coral reefs—with your mask properly secured.

THE END

To read another adventure, turn to page 11.
To learn more about Coral Reefs, turn to page 99.

The boat quickly reaches the patch reef to the right. You strap on your oxygen tank and fins and put on your mask securely.

"Go ahead," Sam tells you, pointing to the water. He still has to finish putting on his diving gear.

Fish swim near a colorful tropical reef.

Turn the page.

You jump in. You don't have to go too far before you see the reef. It's beautiful. Fish of all kinds swim all around it. In another minute, you see Sam. But instead of coming down to the reef, he's motioning for you to come toward him. You swim over and follow him as he goes back to the boat. When you reach the surface, you take off your mask. You hear loud sirens blaring on the shore.

"What's that noise?" you ask.

"That's why I came to get you out," Sam said. "It's a tsunami warning."

"A tsunami!" you exclaim. You know how powerful one can be.

Sam tells you that the warning means there's been an earthquake somewhere in the Pacific Ocean, which can cause a tsunami.

"It's hard to know if one will actually hit Hawaii," he says. "But we should get back to Oahu and find some high ground."

You're glad Sam heard the warning before he came into the water. You hate to think that you could have been out there during a tsunami.

When you get back to Oahu, you learn the warning was a false alarm. You breathe a sigh of relief and look forward to getting back out there to help save the super corals.

THE END

To read another adventure, turn to page 11.
To learn more about Coral Reefs, turn to page 99.

Dr. Johnson introduces you to a scientist named Dr. Tai Ming.

"Dr. Ming has been studying our work here at Carrie Bow Cay," Dr. Johnson says. "But he's going home to Singapore tomorrow."

"Yes, and I'd love you to help with our cleanup efforts there," Dr. Ming says.

The next morning, you and Dr. Ming begin the long trip to Singapore. On your flight, he tells you more about the work his team is doing.

"Other scientists and I started this cleanup effort," Dr. Ming says. "We know how garbage in the water can affect the reefs and other sea life."

"What have you found that can hurt the reefs?" you ask.

"More than half of what we collect is plastic," Dr. Ming says.

Turn the page.

Workers clean garbage and plastic off of a beach.

"In one year, we removed about 1,500 pounds of plastic in just one small area," Dr. Ming continues. "Of course, we find other things too. We've even found a washing machine!"

Soon after you land in Singapore. Dr. Ming takes you out to his research center. He tells you that his main work is trying to start new coral reef colonies.

"How do you do that?" you ask.

"We take small pieces of reef and then grow them in our lab," he says. "When they form small colonies, we bring them back into the water. We attach them to cement sea walls around one of the islands nearby. That way, we don't lose reefs in the area. We've had great success building new reefs this way. I'll show you."

You follow Dr. Ming to a dock. "We have some colonies to transplant today," Dr. Ming says. "You can help."

Inside a boat, there is scuba gear. You both put on the gear as the boat's pilot heads out in the water. Soon the pilot pulls up by a sea wall on a small island. Dr. Ming dives in, carrying a small pail filled with corals. You dive in after him. You watch him use a special cement to attach one coral after another to the sea wall. Then, he hands you the pail.

"Give it a try?" Dr. Ming asks. "Take these, and I'll go get more on the boat."

You take the pail and cement. Then you carefully put some of the cement on the sea wall, just as Dr. Ming had done. You place a small coral colony on the wall.

Turn the page.

This is incredible, you think. You're actually building a new coral reef!

As you work, you spot something moving in the water near your feet. You shine down your flashlight, but you don't see anything. A few seconds later you feel something in the water. You shine your light again.

A diver clears debris from a coral reef off the coast of China.

This time, you see something about 5 feet long. When you spot the fin on its back, you know what it is—a shark!

You take a deep breath. You know sharks don't usually attack unless they feel threatened. You could ignore it and hope it goes away. But maybe to be safe, you should go back up to the surface.

To ignore the shark, turn to page 92.
To head to the surface, turn to page 95.

With your flashlight, you clearly see the shark's fin. You notice it has a black tip. You try to breathe slowly, but your heart is racing. The shark swims around the edge of the sea wall. You don't know if it would attack you if you move, but you don't want to take the chance. You stay completely still.

Finally, after a few seconds, the shark swims away. Your legs start shaking as you watch Dr. Ming return to the water and head toward you. When he reaches you, he can tell you're upset.

"What happened?" he asks. "Are you all right?"

You can only spit out, "Shark!"

"You saw a shark?" he asked.

A blacktip reef shark swims near a reef.

"It swam right by me!" you say.

"Was part of its fin black?" Dr. Ming asks. You nod.

"That's a blacktip reef shark," he says "We have lots of them around here. They're mostly harmless."

Dr. Ming seems to think nothing of being so close to sharks, but you're still shaking. When Dr. Ming asks if you'd like to go back to the boat, you quickly say yes. Maybe you can help transplant more of the corals tomorrow.

THE END

To read another adventure, turn to page 11.
To learn more about Coral Reefs, turn to page 99.

You begin to slowly swim away from the sea wall. You could go faster, but you don't want to let go of the pail with the corals inside. The shark notices you and comes closer. It begins to circle around you. You swing the pail to try to keep it away. But instead of scaring off the shark, it swims closer.

"Go away!" you scream, as you breach the surface of the water. But with your scuba gear on, you doubt it even heard you.

In a flash, the shark moves toward the pail. Before you can move, you feel the shark bite your arm. Your diving suit helps protect you, but you let go of the pail. The shark swims off after it. Just then you see Dr. Ming return.

"I saw what happened," he says. "That was a blacktip reef shark. They usually don't bother people. They rarely bite."

Turn the page.

A diver swims near two Caribbean reef sharks.

"I know," you say, as you show Dr. Ming the teeth marks on your arm. "I guess I just made it mad when I swung my pail."

"Most likely," Dr. Ming says. "Let's get you back to shore. We should have a doctor take a look at that bite."

You go with Dr. Ming back to the boat. There, you check your arm. The bite isn't bad. You're glad you weren't seriously hurt. But the coral you were collecting are gone. You wish you had stayed calm around the shark.

THE END

To read another adventure, turn to page 11.
To learn more about Coral Reefs, turn to page 99.

Aerial view of the Great Barrier Reef

CHAPTER 5

PROTECTING CORAL REEFS

Today, about 5,000 different coral species live in the world's waters. Many people think coral reefs are found only in warm, shallow waters. But about half of coral species live in cold, deep waters. Many also form mesophotic reefs, in depths of about 100 to 500 feet. Reefs can stretch out for hundreds or even thousands of miles. The world's largest reef is Australia's Great Barrier Reef. It is about 1,400 miles long and can be seen from space.

Although many people realize the value of coral reefs, human activity is a direct threat to them.

Over the last 50 years, about half of the known coral reefs have died. Some scientists think the ones still left might die before the end of the 21st century. Some coral reefs are lost because of building along shorelines. Pollution in many forms, from plastic garbage to human waste, can also damage reefs.

A major concern today is climate change. When humans burn certain fuels, carbon dioxide and other gases enter the air. Over time, these gases have caused temperatures across the planet to rise. Ocean temperatures are rising too. This is also killing off some coral reefs.

Warmer waters kill the algae most corals need to live. As the reefs die, they lose their color and turn white. This process is called bleaching. Climate change has also increased the acid levels in the water. Higher acid levels damage reefs.

Some reefs face threats from species that are not native to their waters. Fish such as lionfish can eat algae that the reefs need to live. Or they eat other fish that help get rid of the kind of seaweed and algae that's harmful to the corals.

The effort to protect the coral reefs goes on around the world. Scientists study why some coral reefs can survive harsh conditions and some can't. To collect samples, they have several tools. Some are hi-tech, like remote-controlled robots and minisubs that can go down thousands of feet. But at times, scientists use simple snorkeling equipment to carry out their work.

Back in their labs, some researchers grow corals. Then they transplant them onto rocks or other hard surfaces underwater to try to create new reefs.

Scientists who study marine life are working hard every day to make sure the world's coral reefs survive the many threats they face.